D1098570

Collins

POINT DANGER

Catherine MacPhail

Illustrated by
Iva Sasheva

79 604 906 6

I hate school trips. I was only going on this one to keep my mother happy. "Try not to get into bother this time," she said as I was leaving. "Make me proud for once."

I always try to make my mother proud! I'm not bad, just unlucky. When something happens, I'm there, and I get the blame.

Somebody kicked the football through the school window. We were all playing football; I just happened to be the one who kicked the ball. See what I mean? Unlucky.

And when the PE teacher told me to throw away my chewing gum, how was I to know it would land in Chelsea's hair? Unlucky, I tell you.

Now I was on a final warning. "Behave, or else, MacDuff!" the teacher, Mr Hoss, had told me. "This school trip is your last chance!"

Last Chance MacDuff, that's me.

So here I was on a ferry heading for some island. It was raining so hard the seagulls were wearing wellies. I was standing on my own, trying to keep dry, and Mr Hoss (perfect name, by the way – with a face like his, he should be wearing a saddle) comes up to me.

"Mark MacDuff! Come over here with the rest of the class or I'll throw you over the side and you can swim home."

No wonder I was standing alone. The rest of the class didn't like me, and I didn't like them. For a start, there were Tom and Alex. They looked down their noses at me. You know their kind. Teacher's pets and all that. They shuffled away from me as if I had B.O.

Then there was Gary Bond. He was never far away from Tom and Alex, always doing what they told him. They said, "Jump", and Gary asked, "How high?"

I wondered if I *could* try to swim home.

Chapter 2

The rain had stopped by the time we reached the island. Mr Hoss said we were marching to our hotel.

"A brisk walk will do us good and there is so much to see on this interesting island."

All I could see were trees and rocks.

Mr Hoss strode on ahead, so he didn't see Tom and Alex dangling Gary over a railing that had a sheer drop down to the sea. They thought it was funny. I could see Gary didn't. He was whimpering.

"Don't be such a baby, Gary," Tom said. "It's only a bit of fun."

They pulled him up just as Mr Hoss came running back. "What is going on here?"

"I tripped," Gary told him.

"We saved him, sir," Alex said.

Hoss patted him on the back. He glared at me. "Now, why can't you be more like Tom and Alex?"

I considered dangling the teacher over the wall.

We saw Point Danger long before we got anywhere near it. A white lighthouse standing on the edge of the rocks, cutting a hole in the darkened sky.

There were signs all around it.

"Why can't we go inside, sir?" Gary asked.

"This place isn't called Point Danger for nothing," the teacher said. "It's just about ready to fall down. So I want you all to stay away from here."

He pointed a finger at me. "And that means you, MacDuff."

As we walked on, Tom gave Gary a push. "Doesn't have to warn *you*, does he, Gary? You're too much of a wimp to even try."

And do you know what Gary did? He laughed. He's scared of them. I would have felt sorry for him, but I had my own problems. I was ankle deep in mud, for a start.

But when I looked back at that lighthouse, I have to admit it gave me the creeps.

Chapter 3

It was raining again when we reached our "hotel".

"This is the hotel?" I asked Mr Hoss.

"It is," he said, without a blush.

"This is a hut. H-U-T." I spelt it out so he would know exactly what I meant. And it was a hut.

"I think it's lovely, sir," said Tom.

"Me too, sir." This was Alex.

"So do I, sir," Gary agreed.

They all looked at me. I said nothing.

Mr Hoss shook his head. "Always the troublemaker."

To make things worse, I was put in a room with the three of them.

Mr Hoss came in as we were unpacking. "Tonight, we're going to have a B-B-Q!"

He spelt it out. B. B. Q. Embarrassing, or what?

"And after dinner I'll tell you stories about Point Danger," Mr Hoss said.

Point Danger. We hadn't forgotten about it. We could see it still against the sunset sky.

chapter 4

When the teacher left, Tom and Alex gave Gary a hard time.

"The stories had better not be too scary for Gary!"

"He'll be up all night with nightmares. He might even wet the bed."

I went outside to get away from them. It had stopped raining. The sky was orange. There in the distance, I could see Point Danger. There was something creepy about it.

Suddenly, I heard yelling from inside the hut. I ran inside.

Mr Hoss ran in at the same time. "What is going on here?"

The yelling was coming from a cupboard.

Mr Hoss pulled open the door and Gary fell out.

He was covered in sweat and he looked scared.

"Who did this?" Mr Hoss yelled.

Tom and Alex were standing beside us. Gary's eyes swept right past them. He pointed a finger at me. "He did, sir."

I ran at him. "ME! It wasn't me!"

Mr Hoss held me back. He didn't believe me. "This is your last chance, MacDuff. You do one more thing, just one more …"

Tom and Alex beamed. Tom put an arm round Gary. "We'll look after him, sir."

"Anything else happens to Gary," the teacher said, looking right at me, "and I will know who to blame!"

chapter 5

I was fed up. I wanted to go home. It didn't help that Mr Hoss and his stories about Point Danger were all rubbish.

"Point Danger caused more shipwrecks than it prevented," he told us. "The first lighthouse keeper was mad. He *wanted* the ships to crash onto the rocks.

"One stormy night, the ghosts of the sailors who had drowned came back to have their revenge. The keeper's body was never found."

Then Mr Hoss added, in a creepy voice, "They say sometimes at night, you can hear those dead sailors singing."

"Teenagers having a party," I said. Mr Hoss told me to shut up.

"Then a new lighthouse keeper came, and people from the island started going missing.

They say he lured people to Point Danger to kill them. He chopped off their heads and hurled their bones into the sea."

"I think I've seen that movie on TV," I said. And I'm sure I had.

"You can laugh, MacDuff, but you won't find any local people going near Point Danger, not at night."

chapter 6

I was lying in bed when I heard Tom whispering to Gary. "I dare you to go into Point Danger, Gary."

Alex said, "Yes, and bring something out to prove you were there."

Then they were both laughing. "He'll never do it. He's too much of a baby."

"No I'm not. I *will* go. You see if I don't," Gary said.

They didn't believe him. Neither did I. You'd have to be crazy to go inside that crumbling old lighthouse.

I didn't care anyway. Gary had got me into enough trouble.

Next afternoon, old Hoss gave us some free time. I sat behind one of the rocks and wished I was home.

I heard Tom and Alex coming along the path behind the rock. "Look what we found, Gary. It's a snake."

"I don't like snakes," Gary whimpered.

"I think it likes you, Gary." This was Tom. "It's going down your back."

I sneaked a look. Alex was holding Gary, while Tom was putting something slithery down the back of his shirt. It looked like a snake to me.

Gary screamed. The boys pushed him away. "It's only a tie. You're such a wimp, Gary. Scared of your own shadow."

"I'm not!" he shouted.

"Well, prove it," they said, and they left him.

I watched Gary. He looked so unhappy, and embarrassed. I stepped out from behind the rock and he jumped.

"I don't know why you even talk to those two."

"You don't know anything!" he snapped, and he stomped away.

I walked the other way. I might get the blame for the snake thing if I stayed. But when I looked back at Gary, he was staring towards Point Danger.

In fact, every time I saw Gary that day he was staring at that lighthouse.

chapter 7

That night, I woke up after midnight. Gary's bed was empty.

I had a funny feeling I knew where he'd gone.

I turned over. Not my problem, I thought, but I couldn't get it out of my mind. I remembered what old Hoss had said: "Anything happens to Gary, I'll know who to blame."

I knew there was only one thing I could do.

I went after Gary.

By the time I was outside, Gary was running along the path that led down to the lighthouse. I clambered over the rocks just in time to see him reach Point Danger.

I called out, "Gary!", but my word was carried off by the wind.

He stood for a moment at the door of the lighthouse, and I hoped he had changed his mind. No such luck. He pushed the door open and went inside.

I began to run then, slipping and sliding on the wet stones. I was stupid to be doing this. When I found Gary, I was going to make him sorry.

Point Danger loomed above me. I tried not to think of all the stories: the ghostly sailors, the serial killer, the headless bodies. They didn't seem so funny now. I opened the door and went inside.

It was as cold as the grave. The wind from the sea roared through the broken windows. I could hear the tide rushing in.

"Gary!" I shouted. There was no answer, only a sound coming from somewhere up above me.

I called his name again. "Gary!"

Something banged again. I peered up the curving staircase. I could see nothing. There was only darkness.

Why didn't he answer me?

Was he up there, playing tricks? No, that didn't sound like Gary.

Or was he up there, a killer's hand clamped across his mouth?

Or was there a dagger at his throat?

Or … I shook the thoughts away. Nothing else for it. I began to go up.

The stairs went round and round and up and up.
I began to feel dizzy. Every so often, I stopped
and listened. There it was again. That sound,
like a bony hand thumping against the wall, the
hand of one of those dead sailors. I almost went
back down.

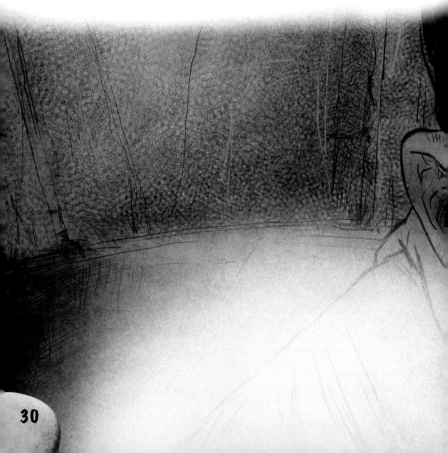

Then in my mind I heard again Mr Hoss saying, "This is your last chance." So I took another step and then another.

I kept calling out. "Gary!"

The wind howled and still there was no reply.

What was I doing here, trying to help a boy who had lied about me? If I had any common sense, I'd leave, right now. But then, I was never strong on common sense.

At last I reached the top, a tiny turret of a room, with broken windows and crumbling stone. Here, in times gone by, the keeper would come to light the lantern that would steer the ships away from the rocks.

But too many ships had sunk, Mr Hoss had told us, and one night the sailors who had died came for the lighthouse keeper. I could almost hear them clumping up these stairs. The keeper would have heard them too, but he was trapped up here. Now, it was said, those same sailors haunted this place.

And the next keeper? He lured people here, cut off their heads and threw their bones into the sea!

Where had Gary gone? It was scary up here in the dark, alone.

Suddenly, right behind me, there was that sound again. I turned quickly. A broken lamp was swinging back and forth, banging against the wall, as if someone had just pushed it.

But there was no one here, was there?

"Gary," I spoke his name again, in a whisper, hoping he would step out of the darkness.

There was a movement in the shadows. I stepped back. My foot slipped and suddenly I was going down, sending stones tumbling. I heard someone scream.

I think it was me.

chapter 9

It was a long way down, but my fall was broken by the stairs. I landed on Gary.

"Get off me!" he yelled.

"I've been shouting! Why didn't you answer?"

"I didn't hear you," he said. "Now get off me!" He gave me a push and I rolled over onto wet rocks.

"Where are we?"

"Don't know," Gary said. "I went up the stairs, and I saw something up there, took a step back and next thing I knew I was down here."

We seemed to be in a cave underneath the lighthouse.

I got to my feet. "Come on. Let's get out of here."

"I can't move," Gary said. "My foot's stuck."

His foot was jammed between the rocks. I tried to pull it free.

Gary yelled. "That hurts!"

There was a sudden rush of waves into the cave.

"I hate to tell you this, Gary, but I think the tide's coming in."

I gave his leg another tug.

Gary shouted. "It's still stuck!"

"I saw a film once," I told him. "Same thing happened to the hero. He had to cut off his own foot to save himself."

Gary yelled even louder. "You're not cutting off my foot!"

The next wave went crashing over Gary's head. I took that moment to tug his leg hard. It came out with such force that we both went tumbling further down the rocks.

"I'm free!" Gary shouted. Then he screamed.

So did I – because we'd both landed on top of a skeleton.

It was a real skeleton: skull, teeth, the lot. Gary began to shake. "One of the victims of that mad lighthouse keeper," he said.

"Can't be," I said. "This one's got a head."
I'm very quick at spotting things like that.

"Then it's the lighthouse keeper who went missing. They said his body was never found."

"So how come no one's ever looked under here?" I said.

"They never knew 'under here' existed," Gary replied.

Another wave crashed in. The skeleton's head turned. It looked as if it was smiling at us.

"We'd better get out of here quick." I tried to lift Gary and he let out another of his earth-shattering yells.

"I think you'll have to carry me."

"In your dreams. I'll go and get help."

An even bigger wave swept into the cave. The skeleton threw an arm across Gary. I've never seen anyone move so fast. He almost jumped into my arms. "Let's get out of here!"

I half dragged, half carried Gary over the rocks until we found the hole we had fallen through. I pulled myself through first, then I reached down to lift Gary.

He handed me a bone from the skeleton.

"What on earth is that?"

"Bring something out, they said, to prove I was here. So this is it!"

"I don't think they meant somebody's leg!"

But he wouldn't give it up.

At last I'd pulled him up, him and the bone. I put an arm round him and together we staggered out of Point Danger.

"There they are, sir!" cried a voice from the darkness.

Alex was running towards us through the mist and the rain. "I told you, sir. It was MacDuff. He dared Gary to go inside."

Mr Hoss was not far behind. He was yelling at me. "MacDuff, this was your last chance! And you blew it."

I looked at Gary, still brandishing the leg bone in his hand. He looked from me to Tom and Alex. I knew what he was going to do.

He was going to blame me again.

Chapter 10

I waited for it. I'd dared him, he would say.
I'd chased him. I was the bad boy. Tom and Alex
looked smug. They expected it, too.

At last Gary spoke. "MacDuff rescued me, sir."

I got such a shock I dropped him and he fell
in a heap on the ground. He looked up at me.
"He should get a medal, sir. He saved my life."

You should have seen Tom and Alex. Talk about jaws dropping. Their jaws hit the floor and stayed there. I only wish I'd had a camera.

So, in the end, I did make my mother proud.

There was even a reward for the skeleton. It turned out it wasn't the mad lighthouse keeper after all. It belonged to a medical school. A couple of students had stolen it for a prank.

They'd planned to sit the skeleton in the lighthouse to scare the life out of anyone who dared to go inside. But the skeleton fell through the same hole we did. That scared the life out of the students, and they fled.

Just one thing still bothers me. No, make that two. What sent that lamp swinging? Was it only the wind? And what was the shadow I saw?

But I'm not going back into Point Danger to find out.

Reader challenge

Word hunt

1 On page 7, find an adjective that means "quick".

2 On page 26, find a verb that means "climbed".

3 On page 44, find a noun that means "joke".

Story sense

4 What sounds did Mark hear in the lighthouse? (pages 30–34)

5 Who did Gary think the skeleton was? (page 38)

6 Why did Mark and Gary need to get out of the cave quickly? (pages 37–40)

7 Why did Gary take a bone with him? (page 41)

8 How did Mark feel when Gary told Mr Hoss he had saved him, at the end of the story? (page 43)

Your views

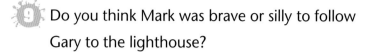 Do you think Mark was brave or silly to follow Gary to the lighthouse?

Did you find the story funny? Give reasons.

Spell it

With a partner, look at these words and then cover them up.

- dangling
- tumbling
- crumbling

Take it in turns for one of you to read the words aloud. The other person has to try and spell each word. Check your answers, then swap over.

Try it

Play the describing game. With a partner, think of as many words as you can to describe the lighthouse. Take it in turns to give each other a word. The person who can't think of anything else to say, or who repeats a word, loses the game.

William Collins's dream of knowledge for all began with the publication of his first book in 1819. A self-educated mill worker, he not only enriched millions of lives, but also founded a flourishing publishing house. Today, staying true to this spirit, Collins books are packed with inspiration, innovation and practical expertise. They place you at the centre of a world of possibility and give you exactly what you need to explore it.

Collins. Freedom to teach.

Published by Collins Education
An imprint of HarperCollins*Publishers*
77–85 Fulham Palace Road
Hammersmith
London
W6 8JB

Browse the complete Collins Education catalogue at **www.collinseducation.com**

Text © Catherine MacPhail 2012
Illustrations by Iva Sasheva © HarperCollins Publishers Limited 2012

Series consultants: Alan Gibbons and Natalie Packer

10 9 8 7 6 5 4 3 2 1
ISBN 978-0-00-746484-5

British Library Cataloguing in Publication Data.
A catalogue record for this publication is available from the British Library.

Commissioned by Catherine Martin
Edited and project-managed by Sue Chapple
Illustration management by Tim Satterthwaite
Proofread by Grace Glendinning
Design and typesetting by Jordan Publishing Design Limited
Cover design by Paul Manning

Acknowledgements

The publishers would like to thank the students and teachers of the following schools for their help in trialling the Read On series:

Southfields Academy, London
Queensbury School, Queensbury, Bradford
Langham C of E Primary School, Langham, Rutland
Ratton School, Eastbourne, East Sussex
Northfleet School for Girls, North Fleet, Kent
Westergate Community School, Chichester, West Sussex
Bottesford C of E Primary School, Bottesford, Nottinghamshire
Woodfield Academy, Redditch, Worcestershire
St Richard's Catholic College, Bexhill, East Sussex